# The Year Jesus
# Was Twins

Julia Cline

With illustrations by Hildy Charboneau

The Year Jesus Was Twins

To the Schellingerhoudts

# The Year Jesus Was Twins

Sometimes it's hard for me to tell whether my mother really enjoys Christmas. When I was little, like my sister, Alyson, I asked Mom what was wrong with Christmas. She said, "I'm not sure, Zach, but I think it just comes at me too fast." That was the year I asked for a bicycle and I couldn't imagine Christmas coming any slower than it already was. I thought she was insane.

Mom begins getting frustrated in October when we go shopping for Alyson's Halloween costume. In October, all the stores make a special place for Halloween stuff, and they start filling aisles with Christmas decorations too. Mom acts like the Christmas aisles are some big, strange dog that she doesn't know. She steers us clear of them. Every year she has the same conversation with the checkout clerk.

"I don't see why you have to deck the halls before Halloween has come and gone," she says, and she's not the only one who feels that way. Usually one or two people in our line agree with her. One year, she even led a sort-of revolt. The grown-ups checking out in the lines on either side of us heard her. They all started asking the

1

same thing. The store manager was helping out with a price check a couple of registers over. A man in that line actually asked the manager about it.

"It all comes down from corporate, you know," the manager explained. "I have to do what they say to keep my job."

"Well then, Merry Halloween!" the man told the manager.

The adults in the lines laughed, and one woman said, "My granddaughter is trick-or-treating as a Christmas Tree this year."

# 2

After Halloween is over—and Thanksgiving—my mom almost seems to like Christmas. She starts to unpack all of her manger scenes— "crèches" is what she calls them. She has the one that her family used when she was a little girl, and a couple that she and my dad bought when they were traveling before my sister and I were born. There are others that friends have given her, some that she purchased from the artists that designed them, and a little plastic one that my sister bought with money from her allowance. That one goes upstairs on the dresser in my parents' bedroom. Mom says it's there because it's special, but Dad and I know Mom puts it way up there because she thinks it's tacky.

My mom likes all of her crèches, but every year she complains about the packing and unpacking. One time my dad suggested that she put out her very favorites and leave the rest stored away. That only made things worse. She talked for two days about which ones she should leave packed and which ones she should put out. Finally, she sat down on the sofa and tugged on the back of Dad's magazine.

"What do you think, Ed?"

Dad kept reading for a moment. Then he looked up at me.

"Hey, Zach, didn't you say we're out of kitten chow?"

"Oh my," Mom said. "I'd forgotten about that." She went to get her coat and was off to the store. Plop and Flop, our kittens, were about four months old and they inhaled food like vacuum cleaners. They ate so much, Mom had them tested for worms, but the vet said they were in the clear and looked at Alyson and me.

"Do they play a lot?" she asked.

"They crash into everything," said Alyson.

"They wrestle all the time," I said.

"Yes," agreed Mom. "Eat, play, sleep; play, eat, sleep; eat, play; play some more, eat some more; play, sleep," said Mom.

The vet scratched Flop under the chin. I wondered how she knew that was his favorite spot.

"You get your brother into trouble, don't you?" The vet blinked at Flop. Blinking is cat speak for "I'm a friend."

Flop blinked back.

"Dad calls him 'The Instigator,'" I said.

"That means he really starts all the trouble, even though it looks like Plop did," explained Alyson.

Mom tickled Alyson under the chin. "It takes one to know one," Mom said. Alyson jerked her head away.

The vet laughed and took a turn stroking Plop, then she let him scramble back into the cat carrier. Meanwhile, the moment the vet turned her back, Flop leapt from the exam table to the countertop and was pawing at the dog treat canister. He was already tipping the metal lid by the time Mom grabbed hold of his middle.

"Quick, Zach," she told me. "Scruff him!"

I grabbed Flop by the skin on top of his neck, like a momma kitty would. He was supposed to go limp. He did mostly, but somehow he managed to knock the lid of the treat jar off and it crashed onto the floor. Alyson stuck her fingers in her ears.

"Sorry," said Mom.

The vet just laughed again.

"We had to put baby locks on the kitchen cabinet doors," Alyson said. She was talking a little bit too loudly. I motioned for her to take her fingers out. "And the closet doors too." Now her volume was better.

The vet laughed some more. When we were at the front desk paying the bill, she brought out a little baggy of cat kibble.

"To tide them over until you get home," she explained. She peeked at the kittens to say good-bye. Then she looked at me.

"You and Plop stick together now," she said. I wasn't exactly sure what she meant, but my mom was laughing.

# 3

So, the afternoon that Dad mentioned we were out of kitten chow, it was no wonder Mom forgot about her crèche problems and zoomed to the store. Nobody wanted Flop to get hungry enough to figure out how the baby locks worked.

Dad stood up and watched out the window until Mom was in the car and on her way. Then he went up to the attic. Flop climbed up the ladder after him, and Alyson followed Flop. I sat on the floor at the bottom of the ladder, rubbing Plop's belly. We could hear boxes scraping the attic floor, my dad's heavy footsteps and Alyson's lighter ones. Plop was on his back, for "maximum belly exposure," as my dad calls it. Plop's eyes were closed, but his ears followed the noises around. Especially the very, very soft patter of Flop's feet.

"Zach," my dad was calling me, but all I could see was a box sticking out of the hole in the ceiling. I climbed the ladder a little ways and brought it down to the floor. For a while, the boxes kept coming. Each one was labeled "CRECHES" in big black letters. Finally, the stream of boxes ended and I could hear Alyson arguing with Dad.

"But I have to find Flop," she whined.

"I'll take care of Flop," said Dad. "You go on down the ladder."

One of Alyson's feet came out of the hole and settled on the first rung.

"But I can help you," she was pleading.

"Down the ladder, Alyson," was all Dad said.

I swung sideways over the floor, so Alyson would have room to pass me. She made her way down, but not without jabbing me in the ribs with her elbow.

"Ouch!"

"If you'd gotten out of my way..." Alyson grumped. She could be a sore loser sometimes.

Suddenly I felt sharp little pricks on the top of my head. Flop was hanging through the hole in the ceiling. Dad had a pretty good grip on him. I leaned into the rungs to steady myself and caught Flop just under his shoulders. He wiggled and squirmed and clawed. I tipped out into space again and couldn't stop, so I had to let go of Flop with one hand and grab the ladder. I tried to pin him against my side with my other arm, but he scrambled onto my chest and up my face.

"Yowee!"

"You OK?" Dad hollered from above.

"Mow-ow." Flop was hanging from the rung just above my head.

"I wasn't talking to you," Dad said to Flop.

"I'm fine," I answered, but then Flop dropped from the rung onto the top of my head. He landed pretty hard.

"Yikes," I said, "He only looks skinny."

Alyson was standing on the bottom rung of the ladder.

"Let me have him," she demanded.

"Alyson, get off that ladder." I knew Dad was giving her the look.

Flop settled on top of my head with one of his front paws hanging down in my eyes. His tail switched back and forth, tickling my neck. At least it was easy to get down the ladder the rest of the way.

When I stepped off, Flop dug in one more time and sprang from my head to the floor beside his brother. Plop immediately started grooming Flop. Plop always groomed Flop after he got into trouble. Mom and Dad said Plop must have been born just a little bit ahead of Flop, because Plop acted like the older brother. I rubbed my scalp, and it dawned on me.

"That's what the vet meant when she said you and I should stick together, Plop."

"What?" Alyson asked.

"Nothing," I said. "I was talking to Plop."

Alyson scowled at me. She didn't like to be excluded, but I couldn't resist annoying her.

Dad was all the way down and folding the ladder back into the ceiling.

"There's five dollars in it for each of you," he said, "If you can unpack all of these boxes before your mother gets home."

# 4

Nothing could make Alyson and me get along like promising money, so when Mom walked in, the family room floor was covered in crèches.

"Merry Christmas, Liz," Dad told her, but Mom didn't look too merry.

"Zachary," she called. "I need your help."

For a couple of hours, I brought her sheep, shepherds, Josephs, Marys, Angels of the Lord—whatever she asked for—until all over the house, nearly every scene was set up just the way Mom liked them.

"Wow! You two are setting a record for the crèche diaspora," Dad commented. He had been playing board games on the sofa with Alyson, so she wouldn't try to help. I made a mental note to google the meaning of "diaspora."

"Dad." Alyson tugged at his shirtsleeve. "Dad!"

She probably wanted to play another round of Hi-Ho Cherry-O, but suddenly—she stopped nagging and pointed at the last crèche Mom and I had left. It was hand-carved, very fancy and painted using only the colors blue and white.

"Where's Jesus?" Alyson asked.

Dad stood up and fake cherries rolled all over the game board.

"Where are the kittens?" he asked.

"Uh-oh," I said, catching his meaning.

"Uh-oh what?" asked Mom. She had been in the living room, rearranging some wise men.

Alyson climbed off the sofa, but Dad grabbed her arm and motioned her to be still. We could hear something rolling around on the hardwood floor in the hallway. The noise stopped and started up again. Mom rushed toward the noise. Dad, Alyson and I followed. We arrived just in time to see Plop smack the blue and white baby Jesus and send him flying. Jesus hit the wall, bounced off and spun round and round.

"At least Mary and Joseph won't need one of those damned rotating crib mobiles." Dad rolled his eyes. When Alyson was a baby, she bawled every time her mobile ran out of juice. Dad had walked back and forth to restart it several times each evening. It really took a bite out of his reading.

Flop put a paw out and stopped the spinning baby.

"Watch out, Flop," said Alyson. "Jesus is probably going to throw up."

Flop pulled the baby closer. Plop trotted over and clawed at Jesus's tiny blue and white head. Flop was not letting go. He chomped down on Jesus.

"Ai-eee!" Mom squealed. Plop's ears went up and he stared at her. Flop took the opportunity to slip between the banister rails and headed upstairs with Jesus in his mouth.

Mom took the stairs two-at-a-time. She managed to pin Flop on the landing. Baby Jesus bounced back down a stair. With one hand still pinning Flop, she grabbed the wooden baby and stuffed him in her pocket.

"Wow-ow," Flop cried when Mom let him go. Plop ran up to groom him.

# 5

From then on, it was like Plop and Flop became obsessed. Wherever Mom set that last crèche, they found it, and baby Blue-and-White went flying around the house. We discovered him everywhere, under beds, in the hallway, beside knocked over potted plants.

"I expected them to go after the ornaments," Mom told one of her friends when she was explaining why our tree had decorations on the top half and not the bottom. "But not this."

About that time, Flop stuck his head out of the top of the tree. Jesus was in his mouth. Mom's friend burst into laughter.

One evening Alyson fished the wooden baby out of Plop and Flop's water dish.

"Oh no!" Mom cried, but before she could get to him and dry him off, Dad grabbed the Jesus from Alyson.

"Let me see this baby." Dad held the tiny carving up and studied its face. "There's been a mistake at the factory," he exclaimed. "This is Moses. Somebody contact the Pharaoh's daughter and see if she's willing to swap with us."

Mom snatched the Jesus from Dad and locked him in her jewelry box.

Alyson was not happy about the baby Jesus being shut up with Mom's jewelry. For several days, she demanded that he be put back in his manger. Alyson is like that—she likes for things to be right and just can't let it go when she thinks they aren't. One time when she was an angel in the Christmas pageant at church, one of the kids that usually went to nursery school crawled into the scene and tugged on a wire that was sticking out of the floor. It turned out to be some kind of hidden extension cord that the preacher could use for special presentations—like when the missionaries came and showed us slides of an orphanage. The little boy pulled until several yards of wire were lying at the foot of the manger. Finally the pageant director sneaked up the aisle and grabbed him. Alyson was standing on a platform behind the manger. She was supposed to be gazing down with adoration at the baby Jesus, but the whole time the nursery kid was pulling, she had her hands on her hips, staring at the little guy's mother. Alyson knew the kid was too young to understand he was messing things up, but she was holding his mother accountable. On the way home Dad changed the words to a carol and sang, "Angels who have glared on high…."

Anyway, Alyson became as obsessed about the blue and white baby being absent from his manger as Plop and Flop had been about batting him around the house. She pestered everyone about it, until, in a fit of exasperation, Mom got creative.

"We can put that manger on the mantel," Alyson was arguing. "Flop doesn't go up there."

"We already have a crèche on the mantel," my mom replied.

"There's room for two. All we have to do is scoot the other one over."

"Alyson," my dad chimed in. "Your mother doesn't want to hear any more about Jesus."

"At least the little blue-and-white one," Mom said.

"Please, Mom," Alyson whined. "Really, Flop doesn't ever go up there."

"Alyson, if we put the blue and white baby on the mantel, Flop will go up there. He's taken the baby from everywhere else we've put that crèche."

"How do you know? You don't know that for sure." Alyson was beginning to sound like she was arguing with me instead of Mom. That could be dangerous.

"Well, it's not Christmas yet, Alyson. The baby hasn't even been born, so why should he be in the manger now?" Mom put her hands on her hips and looked down at Alyson the same way that Alyson had glared at that nursery kid's mother. Alyson sat down on the sofa beside Dad. Mom had that tone we all knew was the first sign of her breaking point. Dad looked at Alyson and put his finger to his lips. Mom went out to run errands, believing she had finally outmaneuvered Alyson.

# 6

Well, Mom's logic was pretty sound, and I guess Alyson decided to accept it, but she had built up a lot of energy arguing about the blue and white Jesus and her brain kept whirring while Mom was away. When Mom got back, Alyson announced that she had hidden away all of the baby Jesuses, every one that belonged to every crèche in the house, even the ones that were stuck to the mangers. She had hidden those, crib and all.

"Because it isn't Christmas yet and the babies haven't been born," she proclaimed.

I looked at Mom. At any moment, I expected her to order the search, but she just seemed to slump under the weight of the bags she was carrying.

"Here, Mom," I took one of the bags from her. Then I raised my voice a little louder and called over my shoulder. " Hey, Dad—Mom needs some help, I think."

Dad looked up from the book he was reading and said, 'Hunh?"

"Alyson has hidden all of the baby Jesuses," Mom told him. I was relieved that she had finally spoken.

Dad walked from crèche-to-crèche, peering down at each one.

"All of them?" He was looking at me for verification.

I nodded.

"OK. Alyson, where are they?" Dad asked, and then we went off on the hunt, while Mom put away the groceries. It was like Flop and Plop had played with all the babies, except Alyson didn't knock over any plants or try to float a Jesus in the bathtub.

The pile of Jesuses on the breakfast table had grown pretty big when Mom came in with a cardboard box lined in bubble wrap.

"We can store them in here until Christmas morning she said.

While Mom carefully loaded each tiny Jesus into the box, Dad looked at me and I looked at Dad. We both knew that Alyson was still roaming around the house, trying to remember where she had hidden the last of the babies.

"Three are still missing," Dad finally admitted to Mom.

She sighed.

"I'll take the womb upstairs to our bedroom for safekeeping," he said, and he picked up the box.

"And you can add the blue and white Jesus," Mom called after him. She looked at Alyson, "So he'll have company."

She sighed again.

"Zach, come help me set the table."

# 7

Alyson remembered where one of the missing babies was during dinner. She remembered where another was during the middle of the night and she woke my parents up when she tripped over Dad's shoes trying to get to the womb box.

The third baby was still missing when the weekend came and Alyson had a couple of friends come for a sleep-over. One of them asked why all the mangers were empty. Alyson explained that Jesus hadn't been born yet and she showed them where the babies were stored.

"This is the tomb box," I heard her tell her friends.

"Hey, Dad," I waited for him to stop reading. "Alyson is saying "tomb box" instead of "womb box."

He shrugged his shoulders," "Well, Jesus comes out live from both places, so we'll just leave it at that." Then he went back to reading. I figured he didn't much want to explain where babies come from to a bunch of little girls.

Meanwhile, Alyson and her friends began to search for the missing Jesus. They started by pulling all the cushions out of the sofa and chairs---except for the one Dad was sitting on. They even faked walkie-talkie conversations like they were real rescue professionals, scouring the side of a mountain.

"No joy in the pantry," I overheard one of them yell.

"Kitchen next," ordered Alyson. "Search pattern alpha."

There was a creak and a thud.

"Ouch!"

"Sorry."

One of them must have yanked open a cabinet without unfastening the baby lock.

It was a while before Mom returned home with snacks and the extra breakfast stuff.

"What's happened here?" she asked.

Dad looked up from his reading.

"Hunh?" he said.

Mom pointed to the cushions on the floor. At that moment, it seemed to me that things around our house would go a lot smoother if my dad were to run all the errands, while my mom stayed at home, but I didn't say that out loud. I just helped stuff seat cushions back into the furniture.

Despite search pattern alpha, Alyson and her friends did not locate the third missing baby. Instead, he turned up a few days later---at the bottom of Plop and Flop's water dish.

"Well, this one can't be Moses or Jesus," my dad was saying as he reached in to recover the baby from the deep. "He doesn't float and obviously, he can't walk on the surface."

Dad stared at the tiny figurine. "Oh," he said. "It's Jonah. We'll have to teach that whale to spit a little farther."

Dad handed me the Jesus and said, "Quick as a flash, to the tomb, my son." I laughed. My mother looked at him kind of funny and Alyson didn't hear a word. She was too busy setting up her own manger scene in front of the hearth.

# 8

In Alyson's crèche, Barbie, as Mary, was draped with a blue cleaning cloth that someone had given Dad at a Christmas long ago. The cloth was for polishing the cars, but my dad, as he said, was "just not a car-spiffying kind of guy." Darth Maul, Princess Leah and Warf from Star Trek the Next Generation seemed to be taking on the role of the wise men—talk about traveling from afar. Also gathered round were a bunch of plastic animals from her collection of toys. She had draped some of my old army men with bits of Kleenex to make the shepherds, and she had raided the medicine cabinet for cotton balls—I guess they were the sheep. I was sure that Mom was going to tell her to take the entire mess upstairs, but instead Mom asked, "Where's Joseph?"

"I dunno," said Alyson. "I don't know what to use for the baby Jesus either."

"Well, just let it sit for a while, you'll figure it out. There's plenty of time until Christmas."

You could never tell with my mom. On weekends she was usually pretty frantic about vacuuming, dusting and picking stuff up. She told us that she had to get the house in order before she went to work on Monday, or she'd just go mad. Then, when you weren't expecting it, she'd grant an exception to her rule of tidy. Alyson's manger scene was one of the exceptions—it sat safely in the eye of Mom's fastidious tornado. And as Christmas neared, we all made suggestions about what lucky toys or household items might play the roles of Joseph and the baby. I offered one of the knights from my castle collection, but it wasn't quite right. Alyson dressed one of her dolls in washcloths and added it to the scene as Joseph, but she wasn't satisfied and took it out. Mom pulled the dish scrubber out of a sink full of water and bubbles.

"Look, Alyson," Dad said. "It's Joseph." The scrubber, with bubbles trailing down, did look as if it sported a full beard. Finally, Dad came in from the yard with a tallish rock. From the side, you could just see the outline of a kneeling man. Alyson was thrilled. She set the rock so that it was ready to adore the baby on Christmas morning.

"Hmmmm," Mom said, when she came in the room to check out the new addition. "So the father is a rock." Then she looked at my dad, who was sitting on the sofa reading another book.

"What?" Dad looked up.

"Mom was noticing that the dad in Alyson's manger scene is a rock." I told him.

"Yes," said Dad. "Strong, solid, dependable guy, that Joseph."

"And also a little hard of hearing, I'll bet," said Mom, as she went upstairs to dust the bedrooms.

# 9

Now that the role of Joseph was filled, we should have focused on who or what would play the part of baby Jesus, but casting for the last role in Alyson's manger scene was overshadowed by another crèche problem. Dad was standing in the entryway waiting to take Alyson and me to our karate classes. (Alyson really likes karate and is good at it. I take karate because Alyson does—for self-protection.) Anyhow, Dad was standing there looking at the entryway crèche. All of its figures are brightly colored spheres about 5 inches in diameter, with small heads and flat bases, so they won't roll around. Dad picked up one of the wise men. There were only two. A couple of years before, when my mom went back to buy the set after thinking about it, the third wise man was broken. She got the whole thing for nearly nothing. Alyson, of course, had demanded to know where the third wise man was. My mom had me read the verses. The story doesn't actually say how many kings followed the star.

My dad picked up the second wise man. He was standing with one in each hand, looking at them. Alyson came running down the stairs.

"What's the matter, Dad?" she asked. "Another mix-up at the factory?"

"No," said Dad. "I was just wondering whether these guys are disappointed. They've traveled so far, and there's no baby to see. Oughtn't we give them a raincheck or something?"

The phone rang. We had started out the door, but Mom stopped us.

"Your instructor has the flu," she said.

I went upstairs to work on my models.

Behind me, I heard Alyson ask Dad, "Which way is east?"

About half an hour later, when I came down for a snack, I nearly fell over the two fat wise men. Apparently the bottom of the stairs was east of their manger destination. I looked into the dining room, into the living room, the family room. All of the wise men were now traveling from the east to their mangers, even Darth Maul, Princess Leah and Warf. Alyson had convinced Dad to put them on the eastern blade of the living room ceiling fan.

"Does Mom know about this?" I asked Alyson from under the ceiling fan. Repeatedly my mother had stressed to us that her crèches were not toys.

"Does Mom know about what?" She had walked up behind us.

"The wise men are traveling," said Dad. He gestured toward the fan.

Mom looked up at Darth Maul, Leah and Warf. "Zach," she told me. "Go get the masking tape."

When I returned with the tape, Mom had Dad looping the cord to the ceiling fan over on itself so that no one would pull it. Then she had me put tape over the wall switch that also controlled the fan. Finally, she turned to Alyson.

"You can move the wise men once a day, so that they get closer to their mangers, but be careful about where you put them."

It felt like we were on the edge of the eye of Mom's hurricane again. One false step and we'd be sucked away by the winds. Alyson rocked up and down on her toes, up and down. She was clearly pleased. I wasn't so sure things would turn out well.

# 10

The wise men traveled safely for about three days before things started to go haywire. Darth, Warf and Leah made it across the blades of the ceiling fan and ended up on the back of the living room couch.

You'd have thought that they were out of danger, but every time Dad sat down to read, one of them tumbled forward into his book or took a nose-dive off the sofa back. Alyson finally wedged their feet in the crease between the back pillows. That worked pretty well until Plop took it upon himself to dig them out. Alyson would stick them in and one, two, three—Darth, Warf, Leah—Plop would pull them out—Leah, Warf, Darth. Alyson and Plop might have gone at it all day if Dad hadn't become annoyed and taken custody of the travelers. He sent Alyson away and sat with the trio in his lap while he read a computer magazine.

Next, the wise men at the bottom of the stairs disappeared. When Mom demanded to know where they were, Alyson opened the broom closet.

"It's an inn," Alyson explained.

"OK," said Mom. "Just don't forget where you put them."

"I have a list," said Alyson, and she held it up in front of Mom. "It's not like the babies though," she insisted. "These guys aren't hiding."

A set of wooden wise men ended up trekking through the limbs of the large ficus beside the dining room's bay window.

"Are you sure they won't fall?" I asked Alyson.

"I stuck them all in Vs," she answered.

I pushed through ficus leaves to take a closer look. For each figurine, Alyson had found a spot where a smaller limb veered off a larger limb. I wiggled them---one, two, three. They were pretty snug.

"See," said Alyson, with her hands on her hips.

"You're right," I told her. "Good job."

It took Alyson a while to reshape her mouth to say thanks instead of arguing with me. I turned around and snorted into the ficus because I didn't want to laugh at her.

"What's wrong," she asked.

"My nose was itchy, " I lied.

So, the wise men were snug in their perches—for a while. Unfortunately neither Alyson nor I had taken Flop into consideration. He was watching the bird feeder outside the bay window. His tail switched.

"Ack, ack, ack." The sound Flop made was the same one Dad made whenever he thought Alyson was taking too many peppermints from the dish in his office.

Flop's butt wiggled

"No, Flop!" Alyson and I yelled, but we were too late. He lunged at the chickadee on the feeder, bounced off the window glass and landed in the ficus. He was hanging from a limb when we heard clunk, clu-clunk, clunk. The three wooden men hit the floor. Flop clawed his way onto the limb and immediately took a flying leap toward the hallway. He dashed between Mom's legs as she came into the room. Dad jumped to the side to let him by.

"What was that?" Mom asked.

"Everything OK in here?" Dad followed.

"Flop forgot there was glass, " Alyson answered.

White sap oozed out of the ficus where Flop's nails had poked holes in the bark. I looked around and picked up two of the wooden wise men. Dad found the third. My guys were OK, but Dad dangled his upside down and its head wobbled back and forth.

"Well," said Dad. "He's not nearly so headless as Nick."

I wanted to laugh, but I waited to see what Mom would do. To my surprise, she laughed too.

"Zach, go get your glue," she told me. I brought down some of the flat toothpicks that I used as applicators for my models and spread a very thin layer of glue in the crack in the wooden wise man's neck. Mom examined the little wooden wise guy very closely.

"Hold on, Zach," she said. "Don't put that glue away." She ran upstairs and came back with a shoebox. It was filled with repair jobs--a chipped teacup, a broken saucer, an injured porcelain figurine, little plastic bits of several colors. I spread the collection out on the breakfast table and began to piece things together. I made sure most everything fit and then started gluing. Before I was finished with Mom's stuff, Alyson brought some wobbly doll house furniture, a few game pieces, a couple of broken action figures—one was mine, but I didn't say anything—and a book that was falling out of its cover. Dad walked up, watched me for a while, and then left. When he came back, he had his stereo headset in his hand.

"So long as you have your glue out," he said. "Do you think you could see whether you can help me with this?" He showed me where the earpiece was cracked.

"Sure," I told him, "but could you scrape all that old glue off first?" Apparently, he had tried to make the repair before—a couple of times.

"Don't worry, Zach," Mom said. "When you're finished with all this, I'll take you to the hobby shop to get some more glue."

# 11

Christmas came a few days later. I don't remember what any of us got that year, but I know that before my mom opened her gifts, she warned us all that nothing would top having the things in her shoebox put back together, and she gave me a hug. I remember that Plop and Flop attacked every ribbon and then crawled around under the wrapping paper. They traveled from piece to piece like big moles. Dad called it "spelunking for house cats."

While Mom and Dad fixed us pancakes, Alyson and I put the baby Jesuses in their mangers. Alyson started to move the wise men back to the crèche scenes too, but Mom said she should wait—because the wise men arrived later.

After breakfast we went back to the tree to clean up the wrapping paper mess. Dad was standing in front of the hearth.

"Oh, Alyson, your manger scene," I said. "We forgot to put a baby in it."

"I don't think you have to worry about that," said Dad. "Come take a look—Jesus is twins."

Plop and Flop had passed out on top of each other, right in the middle of Alyson's manger scene.

Dad, Alyson and I automatically stopped talking. Dad tapped my shoulder and mouthed, "Mom." I moved slowly into the hall and waved Mom out of the kitchen.

"What?" she asked.

I put my finger to my lips and kept waving her onward. When we reached the door to the living room, Dad put his hands in front of his face—like he was snapping a photo. Mom turned back and quietly dug her phone out of her coat pocket. She handed it to Dad.

In our house, moments when the kittens slept were like mini meditations— we all dropped what we were doing to watch their little bellies rise and fall and wondered at how they wrapped around each other to merge into one soft, furry mass, with two sets of ears.

Dad stepped a little closer to the kittens. Then he leaned over the crèche and clicked the phone. Alyson pulled his sleeve. She motioned us all away and knelt in front of the hearth.

After she clicked, she handed the phone to me and carefully stepped onto the bricks behind the sleeping kittens. She crouched down and smiled. Plop stirred just long enough to give Flop's head a few licks. When he was finished, I clicked. Mom tapped my shoulder for her turn.

There was a long pause while Mom thought about her shot. I was worried the kittens would wake before she clicked. Alyson tried to get the phone from her to take another picture, but Mom shooed her away.

Finally, Mom stooped all the way to the floor at the far end of the hearth and clicked. Dad gave Alyson a hug and whispered, "Good work." Flop stirred and his back paw knocked over a shepherd. All four of us stood there, watching the kittens' bellies go up and down for just a moment longer. Alyson was trying to get the phone from mom again when it rang.

"It's Grandma Clark," she said. She walked away to talk. A floorboard creaked.

Flop flipped completely over and took out the rest of the shepherds. Plop lifted his head. It was like he had radar for Flop's mishaps—but Flop was out of reach, so Plop reached a paw out and snagged Mary's long blond hair. He rolled over and tried to groom it. When it wouldn't stay where he put it, he chomped down on Barbie Mary's head. Dad reached down to rescue her.

"So much for 'fear not'," he said.

Alyson started righting the shepherds. Flop stood up and bowed down into a long stretch. He was getting big. His stretches were  much longer that Plop's, but somehow he still seemed to weigh less. His body floated back up into a standing position. Gravity was not an issue for Flop.

Mom and Dad  pretty much agreed that Plop and Flop had finally solved Alyson's casting problem, but, of course, she wasn't sure about Jesus being twins, so a couple of weeks later, when we were at church, Alyson asked Pastor Mark about it. He said that because the birth of Jesus had always been difficult for some people to accept and that it generated a lot of questions—like the one she was asking—he thought Plop and Flop had played it about right.

"You mean just because I'm asking you about it makes it OK for Jesus to be twins? That doesn't make sense." Alyson looked at me and I shrugged.

"Thus, the birth of Jesus remains a mystery of faith for all the ages!" It was Dad. He walked up behind me and put his hands on my shoulders. "I guess you're being updated on our crèche crises."

Pastor Mark nodded and held his hand out for a shake.  Dad took it. Pastor Mark shook my hand too.

"Do you have any questions about Jesus being twins?" Pastor Mark still had hold of my hand.

"Nope," I said.  Mostly I just wanted him to let go.

"Tell me, Alyson," he was looking at her now, and I had my hand back. "Did all of the wise men make it to see their babies without any more mishaps?"

"Pretty much, " Alyson answered.

"Except for the one you left in the pocket of your jeans," I reminded Alyson.

"Oh, yeah," said Alyson. "He went through the washing machine—but Mom heard him bumping around in the dryer before he melted."

"I'm relieved to hear that," said Pastor Mark. "Will they be returning home by a different path?"

Dad grabbed Alyson's hand.

"Oh, yes," Dad said. "They're returning through the land of 'Attic' by way of 'Box'."

Pastor Mark chuckled. "It seems that your family has had quite an Advent this year."

"That's the way I like it," said my mom. "Lots of Advent with a little bit of Christmas on top."

"Hunh?" Alyson looked confused, but, all of a sudden, I got it.

"The waiting, Alyson," I said. "That's what Mom thinks is important. It's why she doesn't like it when the stores put out Christmas decorations before Halloween."

"Exactly," said Mom.

"Everything in its own time," said Pastor Mark.

# 12

After church Mom and I started packing the crèches. I brought her sheep and shepherds, Josephs, Marys, and the angels, one manger scene at a time. Alyson brought the babies and the wise men.

"She's been moving them around so much," Dad had argued. "You can hardly tell her she can't help." He was already unpacking a new book he had received in the mail the day before.

"No more Hi-Ho-Cherry-O for your dad." Mom whispered to me.

Alyson skipped off to get the babies and wise men from the next manger scene.

"So what do you think about Jesus being twins?" I asked my mom.

"Hmmm," she tilted her head to the side and looked at the floor. Dad always said her brain didn't work unless it was sideways.

Finally, she asked me, "Remember when Plop had to wear that cone?"

I nodded.

When Plop and Flop first came to live with us——when they were really small——Plop had to wear a cone around his neck to keep him from scratching his eye. Unfortunately, Flop figured out how to pull at the string to untie it, so Mom shut Plop in the guest room.

"Just for a couple of days, " she had stooped down to tell Flop, but the moment the door closed, separating the two kittens, Flop cried and scratched at the gap between the bottom of the door and the floor. It was awful to watch. Dad said Flop would stop in a little while, but Flop kept it up for twenty minutes. Plop tried reaching under the door to comfort Flop, but that only made Flop scratch harder. Finally, when Flop did stop scratching, he stood at the place where the door meets the frame, the side that opens, and he wailed the hollowest and saddest wow-ows I have ever heard.

It was Dad who gave in first: "Liz! Liz! Is there a way to tie this so, Flop can't get at the string?" He had entered the guest room to take another look at Plop's cone.

Mom came running. She scooped up Flop in the middle of a wail. She called to me over her shoulder as she opened the door, "Zach, get me the masking tape."

Alyson had looked at me and I looked at Alyson. Just that morning we had signed into our e-games as "Tape" and "Ketchup." My parents didn't even know they had made the tape and ketchup assignments permanent. Flop wailed an even longer wo—ow—ow—ow—wow. I figured he and Plop had more secrets than Alyson and me because they were exactly the same age——and both boys. Mom handed Flop to me. I sat on the bed beside her while she taped the string down, way inside Plop's cone. Flop did not want to stay in my lap. Alyson sat by me. She rubbed his head and scratched him under the chin. He kept squirming.

"Let him see, Plop," Dad suggested. Mom and I turned so that the kittens could face each other. Plop was still purring. Flop joined in and squirmed a little less. Alyson put her whole hand on Flop's back. His purr was loud and strong and it came in waves. Dad put a hand on Plop, to hold him while Mom finished taping the string. Dad's hand just about covered Plop's whole body. Plop's purr was a steady rumbling stream.

"If not identical, these twins surely are connected," Dad commented as Mom pressed down the last piece of tape

"OK," said Mom. "Hands off." Flop and Plop headed straight for each other. The cone wobbled back and forth while Plop groomed Flop.

So after thinking about the kittens and the cone, I told Mom, "Jesus had to be twins".

She nodded and smiled. "I think Christmas is mostly about how all of us care about each other. We don't do well without being connected."

I placed the blue-and-white Jesus into a little bubble wrap bag we had saved from a Christmas present the year before.

Plop was rubbing against my knee. True to his name, he dropped to the floor for a belly rub.

"So are you really happy with the teacup I fixed?," I asked Mom. She didn't say anything—she just leaned forward and gave me the best hug ever.

As Mom let go of me, Alyson handed her the rock Joseph. "We should pack him too."

"Of course," said Mom. She swaddled Joseph in bubble wrap and put him in a box. She pushed the box toward me. Plop jumped up and over the box, all in one motion.

I wove one end flap over one side flap, and under the other. Alyson sat down to help. She pushed and pulled the side flaps so I could weave the second end flap under and then over, without the first one coming out.

"Thanks," I said.

"You're welcome," said Alyson. I had to admit I was a little surprised that she wasn't being a pain. It was like Alyson's moving the wise men around had moved her to a different place too.

After a while, I switched to helping Mom pack, and Alyson ran back and forth to bring the crèches and all their figures. When there were no more crèches for Alyson to bring, Dad patted the sofa and Mom sat with him. They watched as Alyson and I packed the last box.

"Let me do the flaps," Alyson requested.

"OK." I watched her weave the first end, and I turned the box around so she could try the harder end.

On her first attempt, a tiny corner of the flap doubled all the way under itself. That made it even harder to slide the bent flap underneath.

"You have to—"

"I know," Alyson stopped my explanation. She straightened out the bent corner and started over.

"You have to—"

"I know!"

I scooted back and sat on my hands to signal that I wasn't going to bug her anymore.

Alyson bowed the part of the flap that was supposed to go under and put a tiny bit of its corner in place. Then—swoosh—the whole flap slid right in. I hadn't even lifted the upper one for her.

"Bravo!" cheered Dad.

Alyson sat on the box to mash the woven flaps flat.

"Be careful," cautioned Mom.

"There's lots of bubble wrap in this one." Alyson defended herself.

"Yeah, lots of bubble wrap, Mom," I chimed in on Alyson's side. I pushed the box toward the entrance to the attic, with Alyson still on top. Mom had never let us pack any of her crèches before. Maybe it wasn't just Alyson that had changed while we were waiting for Christmas.

At the base of the attic ladder, stretched out on top of another packing box, was Plop. He had put his entire front leg through the center where the flaps met,

"Is he stuck?" asked Alyson. She started to move toward the box, but Mom got up and put a hand on her shoulder.

"I doubt it," said Mom.

Dad walked over to start putting the boxes into the attic, but he stopped.

Now Plop was clawing the edges of the flaps with his hind paws and trying to get his other front leg into the box.

Suddenly, he jerked upward, pulled out and sat on the corner of the box, away from the flaps' center.

Flop's foreleg rose from the center of the box.

"Second coming?" asked Dad.

"Water ballet," said Mom. Dad nodded.

"We packed, Flop!" Alyson laughed.

The leg went back in and Flop's head popped up. He looked around like some kind of packing box periscope. Plop leaned forward and groomed the inside of Flop's ear, until Flop pulled the rest of himself out of the box and bounced down the hall sideways. Plop took the bait and chased him.

# 13

Now that Flop and Plop are grown, they don't play with the blue and white baby so much. But when we get the crèches out, Mom and Dad and Alyson and I look at the tiny tooth marks all over their Jesus.

"Plop and Flop were so small," Alyson says.

"Yep," agrees Dad.

"And they were the best Jesus you've ever had in your manger scene," I tell Alyson. Then I think about how she became less annoying that year.

Mom holds the blue and white Jesus and turns him over and over. "He's much more precious with all the teeth marks," she tells us.

Dad dusts off the rock Joseph with his blue car-cleaning cloth. "This year, maybe we'll find a rock Mary to join Joseph."

Alyson nods.

The last thing that my mom and I do is arrange my favorite crèche on our mantel. It's really four framed photos from the year Jesus was twins. Dad named them. There's the "Aerial View" that he took—it's the best shot of Plop's belly and upside down head. Then there's Alyson's shot, the "Classic Panoramic View." You can see all the players, from blue-shrouded Barbie to the very last Kleenex-covered army man. Dad calls my shot "The Artist and Her Masterpiece." When it comes out—Mom always pauses to compare Alyson then to Alyson now—like we look at the tiny teeth marks on the blue and white Jesus and remember the kittens. But the photo I like very best is the one Mom took from the end of the hearth.

At the front of the picture, Flop's hind paw is resting among the toppled army-men shepherds. His toes look huge and the army men left standing look overwhelmed—like someone was filming a sci-fi movie. Further in, you see Plop's belly. It's soft—plush even—except for the individual tabby hairs that stick out of his undercoat. You can see every one of the tiny spikes—as if Mom was using some kind of special camera lens. Barbie Mary's feet and hands are sticking up behind Plop's head. Flop's front leg is lying across Plop's chest like an arm, and his nose is buried under Plop's neck. Along the side are our sock feet—Dad's, Alyson's and mine. And way, way back, between Plop's ears, is the rock Joseph, watching over it all.

Dad didn't know what to call the last photo. The first year Mom put the pictures on the mantel, Alyson tried to name it, but nothing she came up with was quite right.

"You just can't force something like that," Dad explained to Alyson.

My mom nodded.

"Yep," I agreed. "That would be like putting out Christmas decorations before Halloween."

# ABOUT THE AUTHOR

Born in North Carolina and transplanted to California, Julia Cline has written poetry, memoir and short stories since childhood. With a biology teacher for a mother and a father who loved to wander the woods on the weekends, she grew attached to the flora, fauna, dampness and shade of the natural areas in North Carolina. Now she explores the dry, sun-filled hills of California. And, as her parents filled their yard with the native plants of North Carolina, Julia and her husband now fill their yard with California natives. Julia also writes and illustrates picture books. Her latest picture book, *Kotobuki*, tells the story of an energetic kitten and the family he exhausts. Both Julia's written and visual work are fueled by her love of the out-of-doors and the beings that enrich her life, be they feline, canine, human, domesticated or completely wild!

# ABOUT THE ILLUSTRATOR

Hildy Charboneau is a fine artist and children's book illustrator. She enjoys living between the naturescapes of Bigfork, Montana and San Diego, California with her husband, Springer Spaniel and Maine Coon cat. Hildy's most recent project is MOM-ME, a children's book about the humorous joys of being a parent.

Made in the USA
San Bernardino, CA
07 June 2018